AUGIE THE MOOSE

HAS A LOOSE TOOTH

WRITTEN BY ROB COLWELL ILLUSTRATED BY HANNAH TUOHY

I want to thank my daughter, Angela, who said I should; my wife, Rachel, who said I could; and my illustrator, Hannah, who said she would.

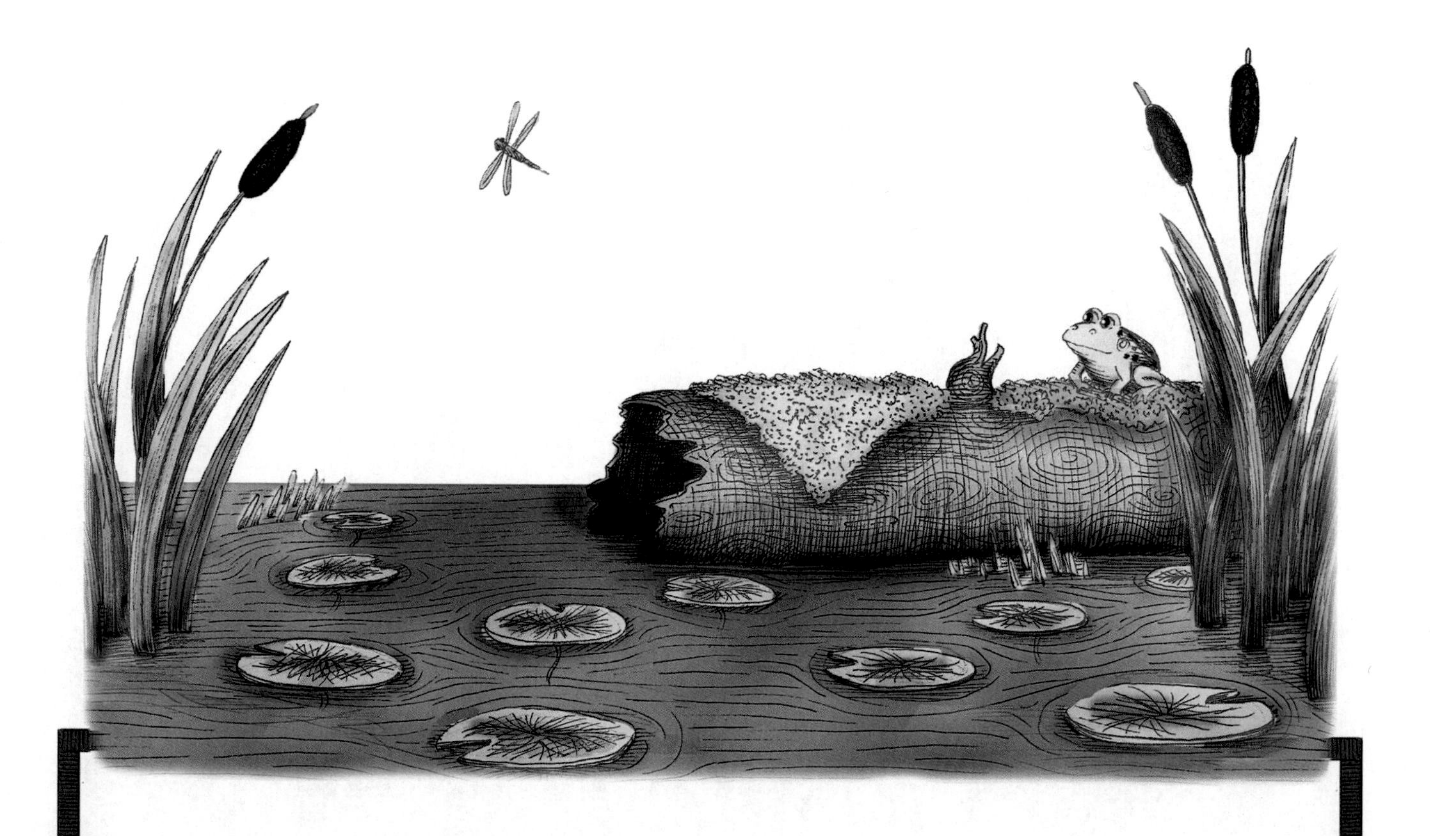

While in his marsh one morning chomping on his favorite greens, Augie the moose noticed something strange.

He noticed some pain in his mouth and realized that he had a loose tooth.

“Well this is no good!” he proclaimed, “Eating greens this way is lame!”

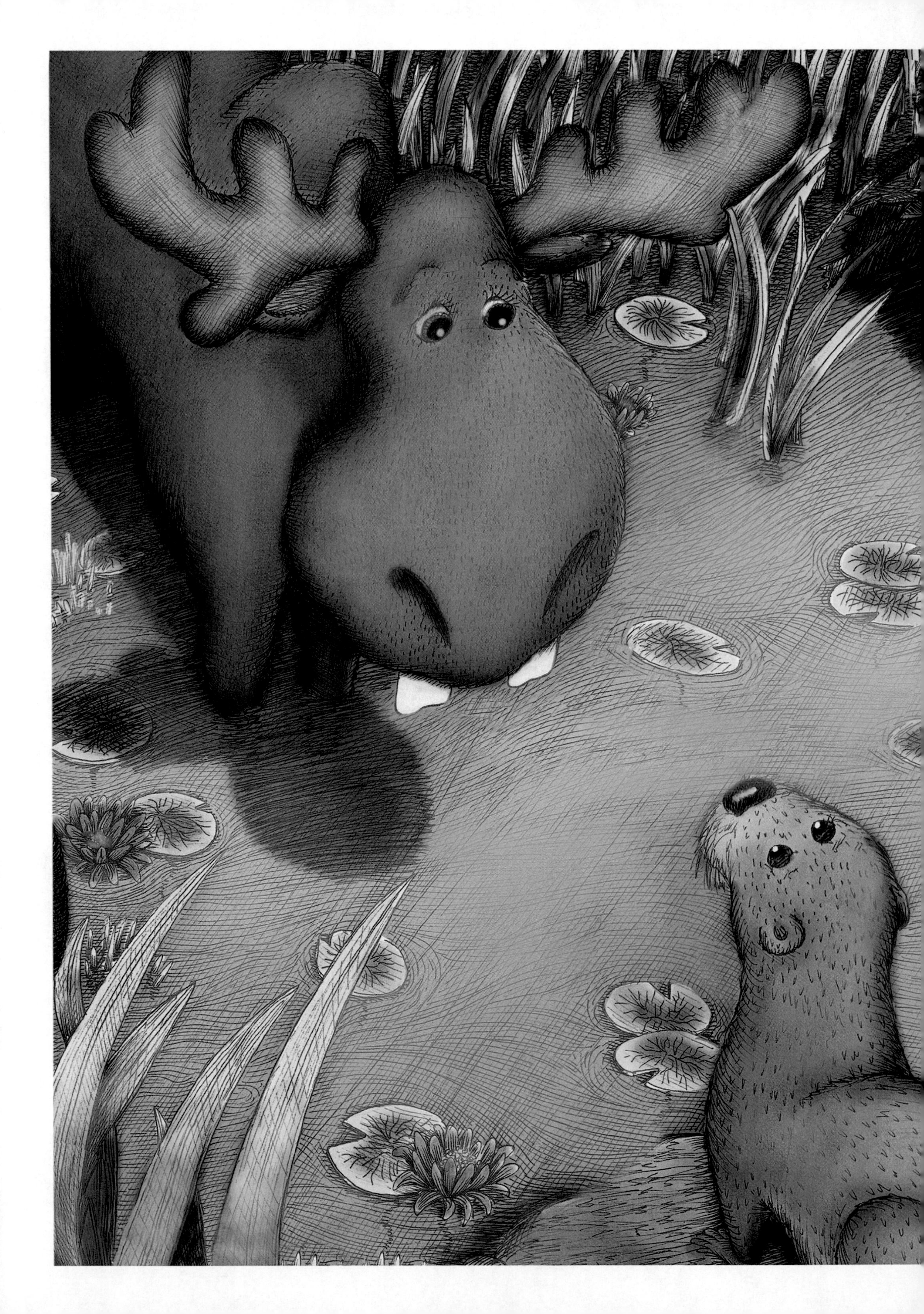

"What to do, what to do, what to do…" thought Augie to himself, when much to his surprise Otter appeared. "What seems to be the problem, Augie?" inquired Otter. Augie answered, "I have a sore tooth – I think it's loose!" "I think maybe," said Otter, "you should go see Snowshoe Rabbit up on the hill. He is really smart and he may know a way to help."

Augie thanked Otter and then headed up the hill. He soon located Rabbit, who was munching on some leaves. Augie explained to Rabbit his reason for visiting and showed Rabbit his loose tooth. Augie asked if Rabbit could help.

"Well," said Rabbit, "I only know of changing fur colors. I know that my fur is a great grey color in the warmer seasons and then it turns a silky snow white in the colder seasons. I don't know, but perhaps your tooth will change as well when the seasons change? I suggest you visit Mama Deer, who lives in the mountains; she has lived there a long time and may know more than I do."

Thanking Rabbit, off went Augie to climb the mountain in search of Mama Deer. Once again, Augie had no problem finding who he had been sent to visit. Standing in front of him was Mama Deer and her two spotted baby fawns. Augie bid greetings to the mama deer. He told her his story and showed her his loose tooth.

After looking and listening, Mama Deer apologized and said that she had no knowledge of such matters. She only knew that her spotted babies would in a short time lose their spots and look like her. "Maybe this is what your fate will hold, Augie," she explained. "In time, perhaps you will lose your tooth like my babies lose their spots. But to be sure you should find the King of the Mountain, the royal Elk. He is old and very wise, having lived so long, and would be a good forest friend from whom to seek answers. You can find him at the very top of the mountain."

Augie thanked Mama Deer and headed out, loose tooth and all, in search of the royal Elk. Up the mountain he climbed. Augie climbed past the field where Skunk once got lost. He climbed past the tree that split during the last big storm. Augie climbed until he had climbed so high he thought he would surely soon touch the sky. Finally, there in front of him stood the royal Elk with massive antlers on his head, basking in all his glory. Augie was in awe of this majestic beast and approached cautiously to tell his tale.

Elk greeted Augie and listened to him tell his story. After Augie finished his tale of the woes of his loose tooth, Elk apologized and said he had no knowledge of such things. "I do know each year my antlers will fall off and a new, larger set will grow back in the next season. Maybe that is what will happen with your loose tooth." Elk told Augie, "Maybe it will just fall off and a larger tooth will grow back." Augie thanked Elk and wandered off in the forest to collect his thoughts and think about all that he had learned during the day.

He tried not to think about his loose tooth, but it was hard not to because it hurt so much. Augie came to a nice, grassy spot under a big tree and decided he needed to stop for a nap. After all, he just had a long journey and he would need to rest for the trip back to his marsh. Augie laid down in the grass and was fast asleep and snoring loudly within minutes, when in mid-snore a funny thing happened.

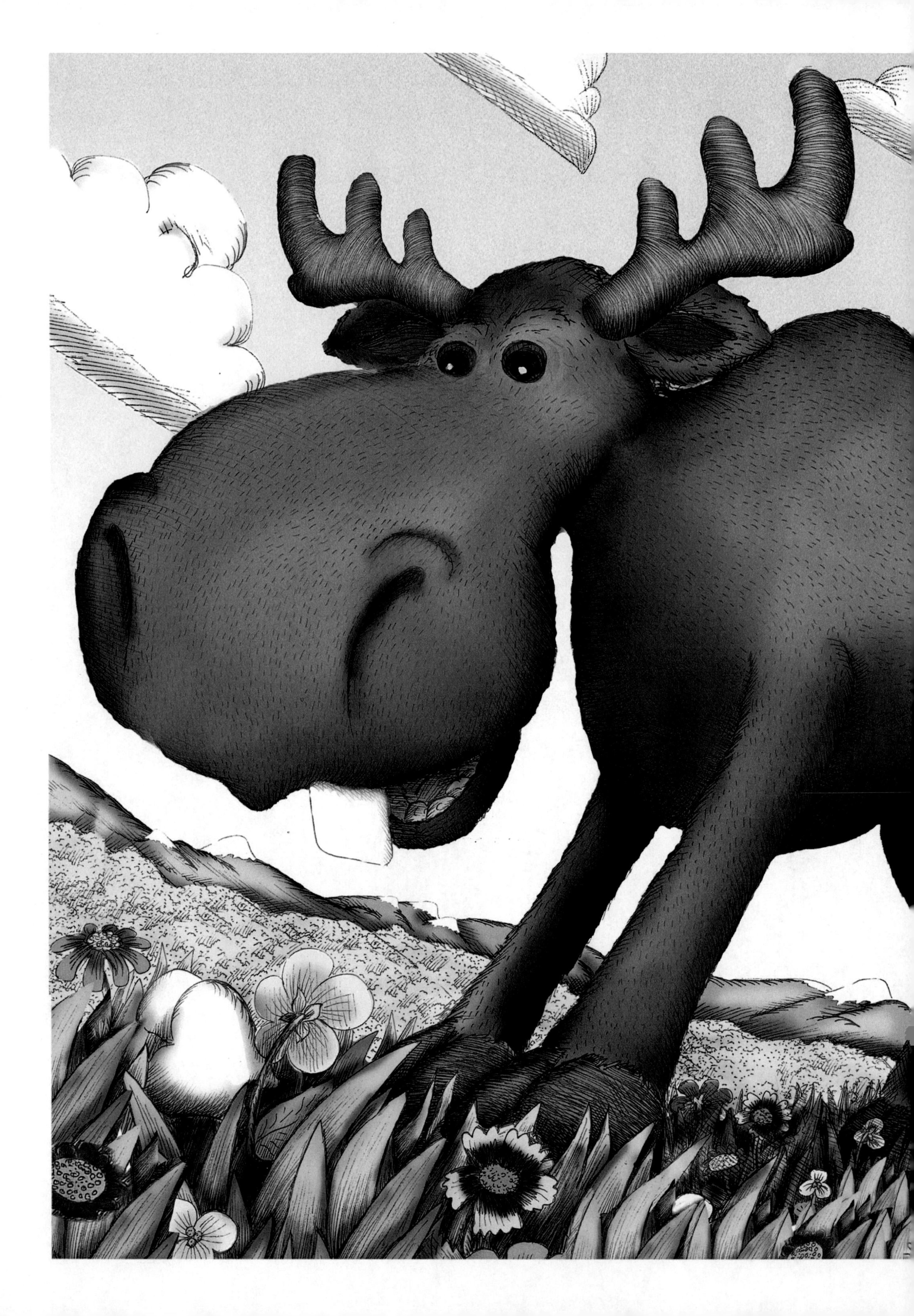

The loose tooth popped out of Augie's mouth and landed gently on the grass in front of him, which is where Augie found it when he awoke.

"Wow!" bellowed Augie at the sight of his tooth lying in front of him. Just like Rabbit changing colors, the baby deer losing their spots, and Elk losing his antlers, my tooth knew just when to take care of itself.

Augie smiled a big, gappy smile not only because he had learned a lot on his journey or because his loose tooth and pain were gone. He smiled a big smile because now he could head back to his beloved marsh and chow down on his favorite greens without worry!

As the sun set, Augie began in a full trot heading back down the mountain towards his home in the marsh and the tasty treats that were in it.

25556400R00018

Made in the USA
Middletown, DE
02 November 2015

MW00956057

Made in United States
Troutdale, OR
01/03/2025